# Walt Disney's Sleeping Beauty

Illustrated by the Disney Storybook Artists
Story adapted by Amy Adair

© Disney Enterprises, Inc.

Published by
Louis Weber, C.E.O.
Publications International, Ltd.
7373 North Cicero Avenue
Lincolnwood, Illinois 60712

**www.pilbooks.com**

Manufactured in China.

8 7 6 5 4 3 2 1

ISBN: 0-7853-9774-4

Once upon a time, King Stefan and his fair queen longed for a child. After many, many years their wish finally came true. They had a daughter and named her Aurora. King Stefan declared a holiday so the entire kingdom could honor the precious little girl. Our story begins on that happy day.

Everyone in the kingdom was bursting with joy. They marched toward the castle in hopes of getting a peek at the beautiful little princess.

*Toot! Toot! Toot!* Trumpets sounded as it was announced that King Stefan's good friend King Hubert had arrived with his son Prince Phillip. The two kings wanted their children to marry someday. The young Prince Phillip stood on his tiptoes to get a better look at his future bride, who slept peacefully in her cradle.

Red, blue, and green sparkles flew through the palace. The three good fairies, Flora, Fauna, and Merryweather, had arrived with gifts for the baby.

Flora was the first to give her present. "My gift shall be the gift of beauty," she said, waving her magic wand.

Next it was Fauna's turn. "Tiny princess," she said, waving her wand, "my gift shall be song."

Finally it was Merryweather's turn. But suddenly the wind howled, the castle door flew open, and there was a burst of smoke.

It was Maleficent, the evil fairy. Everyone knew she was wicked. "I would like to give the child a gift, too," Maleficent cackled. "Before the sun sets on her sixteenth birthday she will prick her finger on the needle of a spinning wheel and never awaken."

*Crack!* Thunder clapped, and the evil Maleficent disappeared.

Maleficent's spell was much too powerful to undo. But Merryweather could help. "Sweet princess," Merryweather said, "if your finger pricks a needle you will fall into a deep sleep. But you'll awaken when you receive true love's kiss."

The three good fairies wanted to break the spell, but they could not think of a way to stop Maleficent. The tiny princess would never be safe.

Then Flora had an idea. She told Merryweather and Fauna that they all could live as peasants in an abandoned woodcutter's cottage deep in the forest. They would raise Princess Aurora. Then on Princess Aurora's sixteenth birthday, when the spell was finally broken, they would return Aurora to the palace.

The fairies told the king and the queen their plan. The king and queen knew it was the only way their precious daughter would be safe from Maleficent. So they watched with heavy hearts as the fairies left with their only child.

Maleficent did not give up. For sixteen long years she searched far and wide for the princess. Then Maleficent sent out her raven to search for the girl one last time.

The fairies lived like people. They feared that if they used their magic, Maleficent would surely find them. They acted as the princess's aunts and called her Briar Rose. As the princess grew to become a beautiful young lady, she began to dream about finding true love.

On her sixteenth birthday, Briar Rose skipped into the forest to pick berries. She began to sing a lovely song. The song was so beautiful that even the birds fluttered around her and whistled along.

At the same time, a young prince rode through the forest. He heard Briar Rose's song and couldn't help but follow the enchanting music. He thought the song was too lovely to be real.

When he saw Briar Rose, he fell instantly in love. The two danced by the pond. Round and round the prince twirled her. It was truly magical— just as Briar Rose had dreamed. She told the prince to meet her later that evening at the cottage in the glen.

While Briar Rose was out picking berries, the three fairies tried to make a dress fit for a princess and bake a beautiful birthday cake delicious enough for royalty.

When they were done, the dress did not look like it was made for a princess. The cake toppled over — it was not fit for royalty either.

The fairies did not want to disappoint Briar Rose. They decided they had to risk using their magic. They shut the doors, closed the windows, and locked up every nook and cranny so no one would see or hear what they were about to do.

With a wave of their wands, the eggs and flour started mixing in the bowl. The scissors and thread sewed a beautiful dress.

The dress was lovely, but Flora and Merryweather could not agree on a color. "Make it blue," said Merryweather, as blue sparkles shot from her wand.

"Pink," Flora said, as little pink sparkles danced all around. The dress turned blue, then pink, then blue, then pink. There were so many pink and blue sparkles that they shot right out of the chimney.

At that moment, Maleficent's raven flew by, right into the sparkles!

Briar Rose was excited when she saw the dress and cake. "This is the happiest day of my life," she said. "Just wait until you meet the man I love."

"You've met a stranger?" Flora asked.

"He's not a stranger," Briar Rose said. "We've met before — once upon a dream."

"But you are already betrothed," Fauna said, "to Prince Phillip."

Briar Rose's eyes widened. "How could I marry a prince? I'd have to be a princess."

The three fairies told Briar Rose she was really Princess Aurora, the daughter of King Stefan. She was to return to the castle that night.

"But I promised to meet my true love tonight," the princess said as she started to cry.

"You must never see him again," Flora said sadly.

Princess Aurora could not stop crying. The news was just too much for her to bear.

Maleficent's raven had heard everything. He flapped his wings and flew off to tell Maleficent. He knew she would be very pleased.

The king, queen, and King Hubert anxiously awaited the arrival of Princess Aurora. King Hubert's son, Prince Phillip, was to marry Princess Aurora that very day. Prince Phillip rode to the castle. He came not to marry the princess, but to tell his father that he had found true love.

"Where did you meet her?" King Hubert demanded.

"Once upon a dream," Prince Phillip said, and he raced back to the forest.

Meanwhile, the three fairies led Aurora safely back to the castle. Princess Aurora started to cry again. She couldn't help but think about her true love. She was sure she would never see him again.

The fairies quietly slipped out of Aurora's room so the princess could be alone. As soon as they left, the fireplace dimmed to a green glow. Princess Aurora's eyes locked on the strange light. She rose from her chair and slowly followed it.

The three fairies knew
something was wrong.
They burst back into the
room. But it was too late.
The princess had followed
the green glow through a
trap door. It slammed
shut before the fairies
could rescue her.

The three fairies waved their wands, and the bricks on the trap door vanished. They quickly raced up the steps.

The princess climbed higher and higher. Suddenly Maleficent appeared. She had a spinning wheel. "Touch the spindle," Maleficent said. The princess slowly stuck out her finger and pricked it on the needle. She fell to the floor.

When the three fairies found the princess, they cried. They knew the king and queen would be heartbroken.

"They'll never find out! We'll put them all to sleep," Flora said. "They will sleep until the princess awakens."

The three fairies fluttered throughout the castle and waved sleeping dust over all the people. Even the guards stretched and yawned and fell into a deep sleep.

Flora sprinkled sleeping dust on King Hubert. But just before he fell asleep he told King Stefan that Prince Phillip had fallen in love with a girl he had met once upon a dream.

Flora instantly knew that Prince Phillip was the mysterious stranger that Princess Aurora had fallen in love with. He could break the spell!

The three fairies raced back to their cottage deep in the forest. But they were too late. They found Prince Phillip's red hat, but he was gone. They knew Maleficent had captured him, so they set out for Maleficent's castle to rescue him.

They found Prince Phillip chained in the dungeon. The fairies unlocked his chains. The guards spotted them and tried to stop the fairies by rolling heavy rocks at them.

*Poof!* The good fairies turned the rocks into bubbles!

Maleficent saw that the prince was escaping. A violent storm started to brew. Black clouds wrapped around the castle. Then Maleficent made thorns shoot up all around King Stefan's castle, blocking Prince Phillip's path. But Prince Phillip was very strong. He cut right through the thorns with his sword.

Maleficent would not give up. She turned into a gigantic fire-breathing dragon. Even though Maleficent was a mighty dragon, she could not defeat the brave prince and the three good fairies. The dragon fell to the ground, and Maleficent was never heard from again.

Prince Phillip raced to his sleeping beauty. He knelt down beside her and gently kissed her. Princess Aurora's eyes slowly opened. With that, everyone else in the castle woke from their deep slumber.

Trumpets sounded. The lovely princess and handsome prince danced for all the people in the palace — just as they had danced in the forest. They soon were married. All of Princess Aurora's dreams had finally come true.